A Hug for Maggie

by Olivia Barham

Illustrations by Karol Ka~~~~~

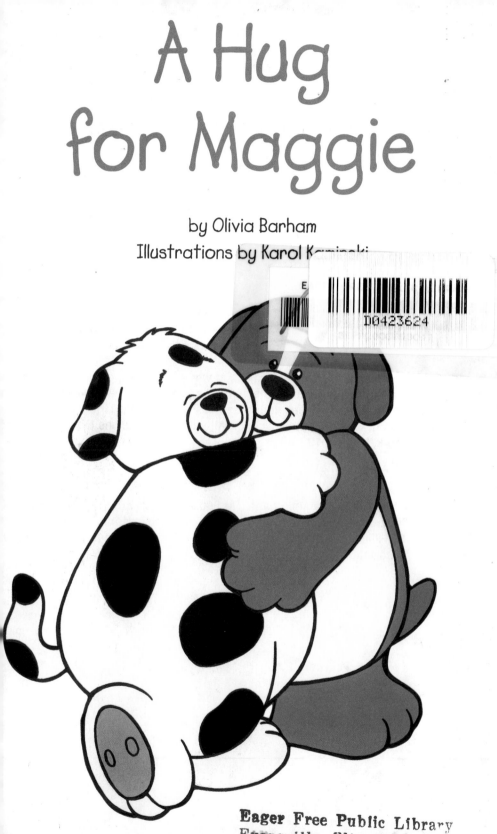

This book is dedicated to Maggie,
whose hugs are as big as her smiles.
— O.B.

ISBN 0-439-35587-7

12 11 10 9 8 7 6 5 4 3 2 1   2 3 4 5 6/0

Printed in the U.S.A.   24

First Scholastic printing, February 2002

Written by Olivia Barham
Illustrated by Karol Kaminski
Designed by Carisa Swenson

Maggie was new in Chubby Town, and she was feeling blue.

So she went to see the doctor,
who would know just what to do.

Dr. Sophie looked
at Maggie's feet,
and chest, and head.

"You do not need to have a shot.
You need a hug," she said.

"A hug?" said Maggie. "What is that?
I just moved here, you see.
This hugging that you talk about
is very new to me."

"Hop on my bike,"
said Sophie.
"I will show you all around.
And you can see how Chubbies
hug, in huggy Chubby Town."

"Okay," said Maggie.
"Will it hurt?"

"Oh, no. It will be fun.
Just look and you will find out
how a Chubby hug is done."

A hug is for saying
"Hello" with your heart.

It also says, "Good-bye."

A hug is for saying,
"Well done! You did great!

Or "Uh-oh.
Do not cry."

A hug can make it better,
if it hurts really bad.

A hug can make you
happy, when you feel
really sad.

A hug says, "You are special."

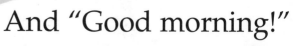

And "Good morning!"

And "Good night."

A hug can stop you shaking,
if you see a scary sight.

A hug is for your friend,
just because she is there.

nd when you get excited,
hug will show you care.

Even if you hug all day,
you never get worn out.

Hugging gives you energy,
it does not take it out.

"Oh," said Maggie. "Now I see.
I bet that does feel good."
So she stood by the road with
her arms open wide . . .

and stood,

27

and stood,

and stood.

But no hug came. It made her sad.
"Do not cry," Sophie said.
"If you really want to get a hug,
then give a hug instead."

"When you give a hug, you get one.
It is the same in the end.
Come here," she said.
"I will show you..."

"That hug said, I love you.
Will you be my friend?"